BABS BUNNY, PRIVATE EAR

This Tiny Toon Adventures Book is published by Longmeadow Press, in association with Sammis Publishing.
Distributed by Book Sales, Inc., 110 Enterprise Ave., Secaucus, NJ 07904

With special thanks to

Guy Gilchrist • Gill Fox • Tom Brenner • Marie Gilchrist
Jim Bresnahan • Frank McLaughlin • Allan Mogel • Gary A. Lewis

Printed in the United States of America
0 9 8 7 6 5 4 3 2 1

BABS BUNNY, PRIVATE EAR

written by Gary A. Lewis

Illustrated by
The *Guy Gilchrist* Studios ™

The whole thing started bright and early one Monday morning. Babs Bunny and Buster Bunny got to Acme Looniversity for their first class, only to find a big crowd gathered around the front door of the school.

"Hey, what's up?" Babs asked Plucky Duck. "You're not going to believe this," Plucky replied. "The old Loo is going to close down!"

"Close down?" Buster said. "What are you talking about?"

"It's true," said Hamton, coming over. "Acme Savings and Loan claims the school hasn't paid the mortgage in months. Acme Loo has been sold."

"No more school," Dizzy Devil added mournfully.

7

"But I don't get it," Professor Fudd was saying to Professor Sam. "I've been sending the money in evewy month."

"Well, sumpin's gone wrong," Professor Sam replied. "And we're in a heap of trouble, pardner."

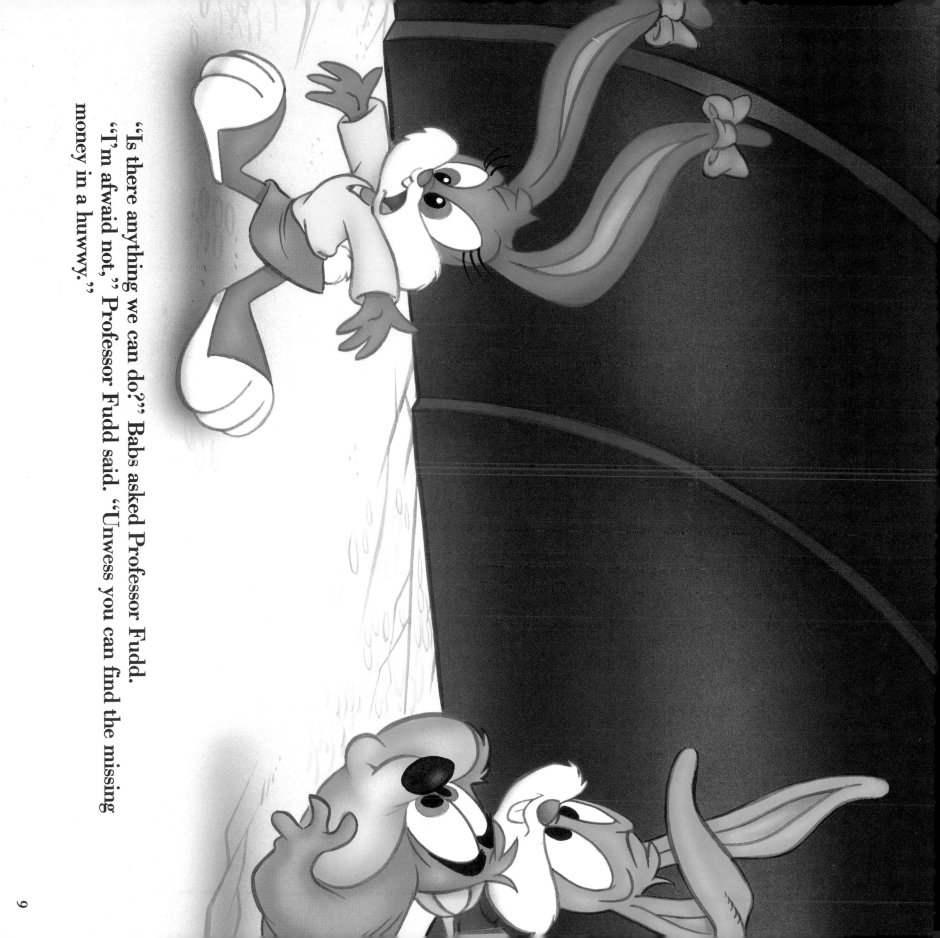

"Is there anything we can do?" Babs asked Professor Fudd.

"I'm afwaid not," Professor Fudd said. "Unwess you can find the missing money in a huwwy."

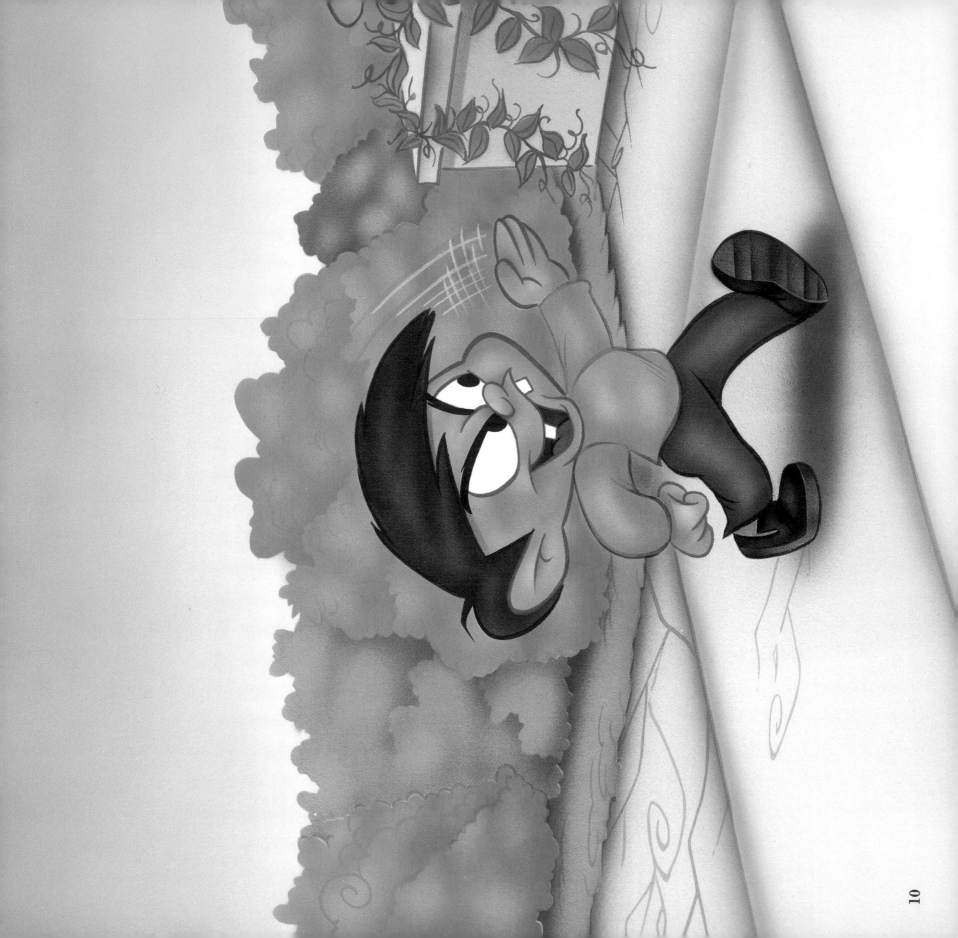

Just then, Montana Max wandered by.

"Hey, did'ja hear the news?" Buster asked him.

"Oh, you mean about our late, lamented school?" Monty smirked. "No big loss. I'm transferring to Perfecto Prep this year anyway. So long, suckers!" And Montana Max walked away, laughing.

"That's rotten," said Hamton. "Doesn't he have any school spirit?"

"That's also strange," Babs said.

"What's strange?" asked Buster.

"That he knew about the school's closing," Babs replied, "without even reading the notice."

"So?" Plucky scratched his head.

"So...this sounds like a case for...Babs Bunny, Private Ear. See you guys later." And without another word, Babs turned and headed down the street.

"Hey, wait for me!" Buster called. "I'm coming with you!"

"Us too!" shouted Plucky and Hamton.

Their first stop was Acme Savings and Loan. There, they spoke to the bank manager.

"Yes, Acme Looniversity took out a new mortgage last year to build a humor lab," the manager told them, consulting his records. "Never missed a payment until four months ago. Then, the money simply stopped coming. We tried to contact them, but there was no reply. So I'm afraid that at noon today, Acme Looniversity will be closing down."

"I don't get it," said Buster. "Professor Fudd said he'd been paying the bank regularly, but the bank never got the money. And I'll bet Acme Loo never got any letters, either."

"And there's that other question," Babs said, frowning. "How did Montana Max know about the school's closing in advance?" Then she suddenly snapped her fingers.

"I've got a thought," she said. She turned to the bank manager. "Sir, do you know who will own Acme Loo once it closes?" she asked.

"As it happens, I do," the manager replied. "The property has already been sold...to Perfecto Prep."

"I thought so," said Babs as she and her three friends left the bank.

"Thought so what?" Plucky asked.

"Montana Max and Perfecto Prep," Babs replied. "It's too much of a coincidence. Somehow, Monty is involved in all this. And I'm going to find out how."

"Speaking of Montana Max," Hamton said suddenly. "There he is!"

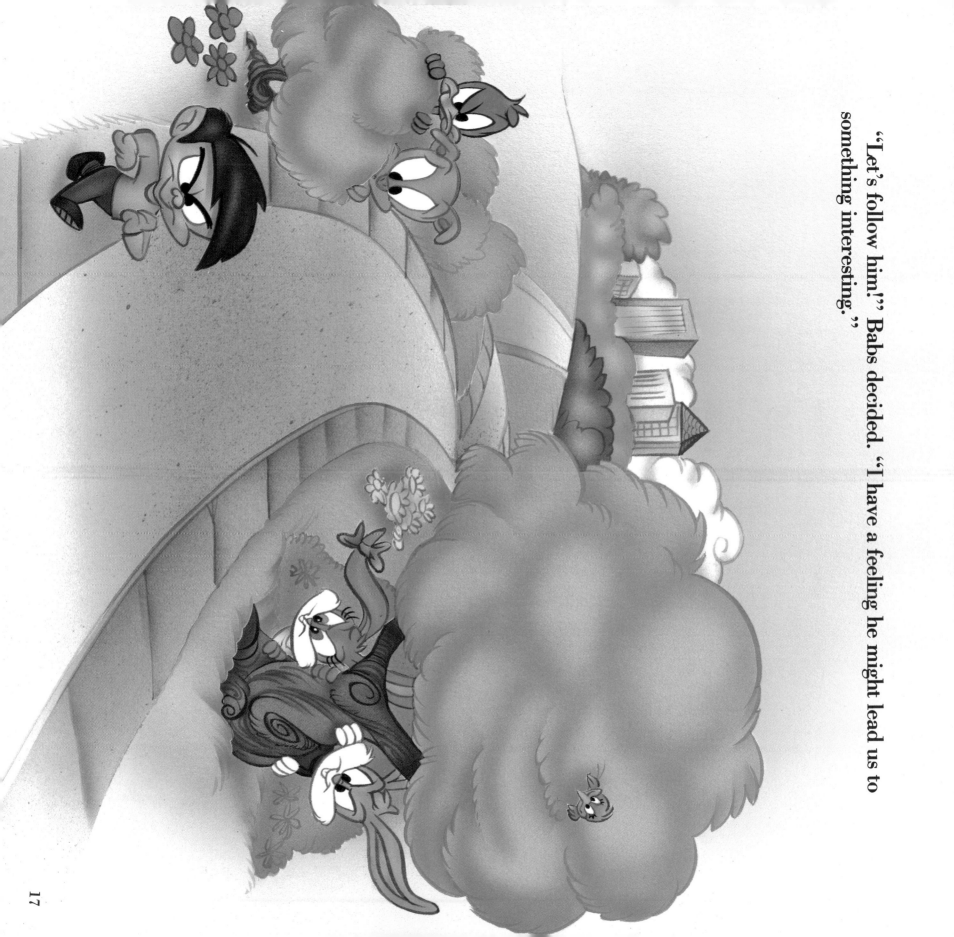

"Let's follow him!" Babs decided. "I have a feeling he might lead us to something interesting."

Babs, Buster, Plucky, and Hamton followed Montana Max to a deserted old house out near Perfecto Prep. Monty looked around, and then quickly slipped in the front door.

"Let's listen in," Babs suggested.

"Okay," Buster agreed. "But we don't have a lot of time."

Babs, Buster, Plucky, and Hamton peered in the window of the house. Much to their surprise, there was Montana Max, talking to the principal of Perfecto Prep!

"Have you got all the money?" the principal asked Monty.

"You bet, sir," said Monty. "It's buried right behind my house."

"Good," said the principal. "I'll pick it up later. Lucky you got that job in the Acme Looniversity office."

"Yeah," laughed Monty. "And would you believe Professor Fuddy-Duddy actually had *me* going to the bank with the money? Stealing it was like taking candy from a bunny!"

Outside, Babs snapped her fingers. "That's how he did it!" she whispered.

"I don't get it," Plucky said.

"Just this semester, that creep Montana Max took a job in the Acme school office." Babs explained. "It made it easy for him to steal the money and destroy the bank's letters. And in exchange for closing down our school, he's obviously going to be allowed into Perfecto Prep!"

"No way they'd let him in otherwise," Buster said.

"Shhh!" hissed Babs. "Here they come!"

"Well, I'll see you first thing tomorrow morning at Perfecto," Montana Max was saying. "Rah rah rah! And by the way...what are you going to do with good old Acme Loo?"

"Oh," gloated the principal. "We're turning it into a giant gourmet food store. You know...duck soup, rabbit in carrot sauce, pig's knuckles..."

"Sounds delicious," Montana Max smirked.

"A gourmet food store?" Plucky gasped. "That's disgusting!"

"We can't let him do it!" Babs declared. "We've got to get the money back!"

"But how?" asked Buster, shaking his head. "We only have an hour left."

"I have an idea, Babs replied. "Now, this is what we do…"

Fifteen minutes later, Montana Max had visitors. They were from the Acme Gourmet Food Company.

"Excuse me, sir," said the delivery person. "Montana Max?"

"Yeah, that's me," said Monty.

"We've got a delivery here. The principal of Perfecto Prep told us to collect all the money from you."

"He did?" said Monty.

"He did," said the delivery person. "Sign here, please."

"Okay," Montana Max said. "If he said so. I'll be right back." And then he disappeared around the side of the house.

After Montana Max had dug up the money, he brought it back to the delivery person.

"Thanks," said the delivery person. "Gotta run!"

Monty watched as the Acme Gourmet Food Company van pulled away.

Just then, the principal of Perfecto Prep drove up.

"Monty!" he said, rolling down the window. "Where's the money?"

"I did what you said, sir," Montana Max answered. "I gave it to the delivery people."

"What delivery people?" demanded the principal.

"The ones with the food you ordered for your gourmet food store," Monty explained.

"You've been tricked, Monty!" shouted the principal. "I never ordered any food! Now there's no money...and that means I can't buy Acme Loo after all!"

STOMP!

STOMP!

STOMP!

Beep! Beep!

In the meantime, the delivery people were far away.

"Whew!" said Buster. "I thought Monty would recognize us for sure."

"Not that dude," laughed Babs. "He's a real airhead. Now, let's go pay the bank a visit and save Acme Loo!"

When Babs delivered the money to the Acme Savings and Loan, the bank decided not to close Acme Loo after all. And when the story got around about Montana Max, nobody sat next to him at lunch for a long, long time. The case was solved...thanks to Babs Bunny, Private Ear!